POW!

Brooklyn, NY

I AM TODAY

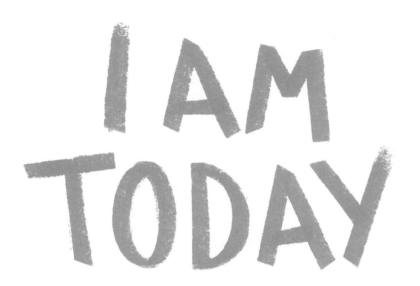

Matt Forrest Esenwine

Illustrations by Patricia Pessoa

Grown-ups say I am the Future.

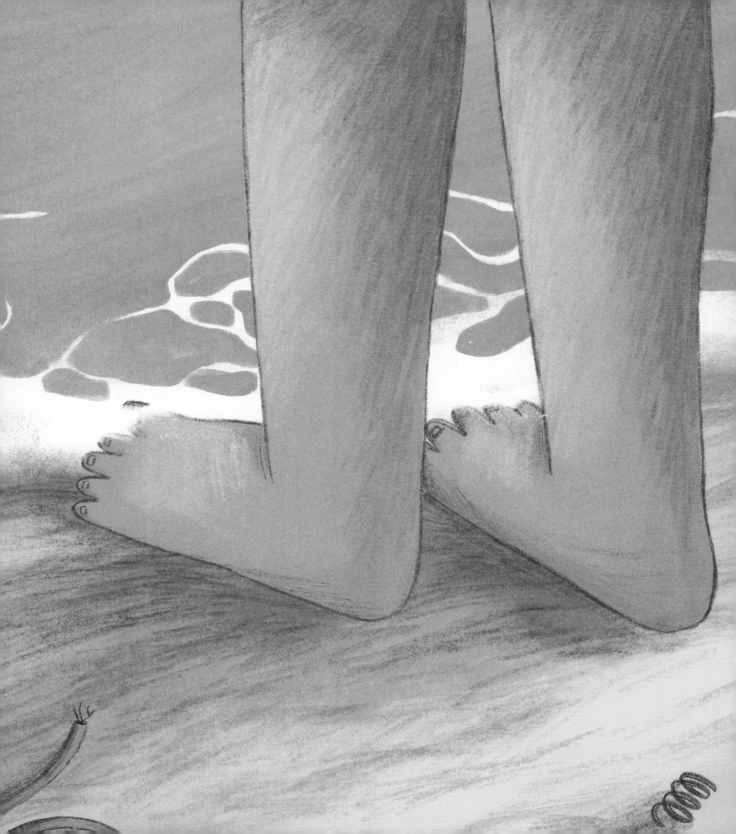

But I'd rather be the Now.

Why wait to make a change for good?
I'm strong.
And I know how!

I've learned from those before me what's truthful.

They've taught me how to be polite.

They've shown me how to share.

If I see something isn't right,
I need to take a stand!

Why wait to offer kindness?
Why wait to lend a hand?

Someday I'll be the Future,
but I'd rather be Today.

I'm needed in the Here and Now —
and not so far away.

I'll lend support.
I'll show great love
in thought and deed and word.

All the world will learn my cause;
my voice, it will be heard!

The past is far behind us,
the future, well beyond.

There's never been
a better time to listen...

...learn...

...respond!

There's still so much I want to do —
so much I have to say!

Someday I'll be the Future.

But right now...

...I am Today.

How To Make an Origami Turtle:

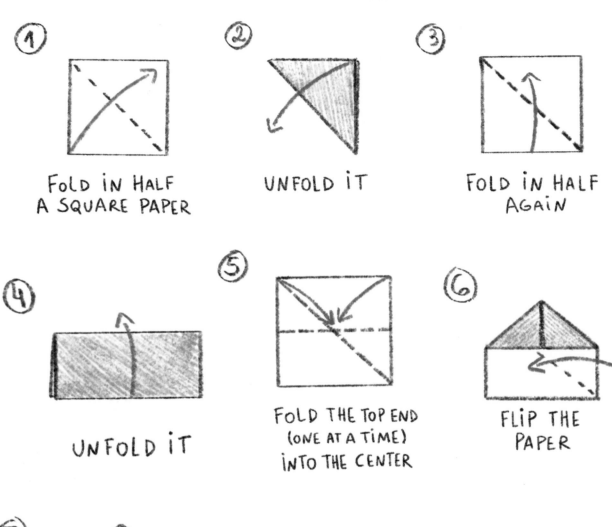

① FOLD IN HALF
A SQUARE PAPER

② UNFOLD IT

③ FOLD IN HALF
AGAIN

④ UNFOLD IT

⑤ FOLD THE TOP END
(ONE AT A TIME)
INTO THE CENTER

⑥ FLIP THE
PAPER

⑦ FOLD THE SIDES
INTO THE CENTER
(USE THE IMAGINARY
LINES AS GUIDES)

⑧ FOLD IN THE BOTTOM
CORNER INTO THE CENTER.

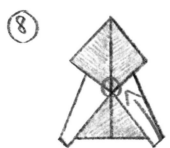

DO THE SAME WITH THE OTHER SIDE

FOLD OUT THE FLAPS FOLLOWING THE IMAGINARY LINES

FOLD THE TOP INTO THE CENTER

FOLD OUT USING THE IMAGINARY LINE

FLIP IT

IT'S READY!

- - - - - - - - **FOLD MARKS**

——————— **IMAGINARY LINES**

"To Jennifer, my Today and my Future."—M.F.E.

"For my dad, who loved Origami." —P.P.

I Am Today
Text © 2021 Matt Forrest Esenwine
Illustrations © 2021 Patricia Pessoa

Published by POW!
a division of powerHouse Packaging & Supply, Inc.
32 Adams Street, Brooklyn, NY 11201-1021

www.POWKidsBooks.com
Distributed by powerHouse Books
www.powerHouseBooks.com

First edition, 2021

Library of Congress Control Number: 2021937046

ISBN 978-1-57687-994-8

Printed by Toppan Leefung

10 9 8 7 6 5 4 3 2 1

Printed and bound in China